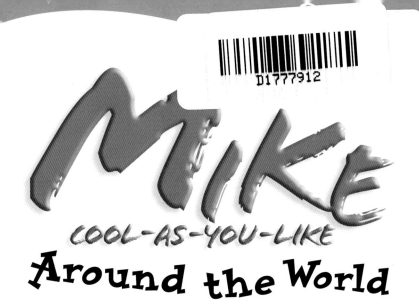

MIKE
COOL-AS-YOU-LIKE
Around the World

JUSTIN BROWN
Series Editor: Joy Cowley

For Jacob H.

Signatures
Mike Cool-as-You-Like: Around the World

This edition published by
Clean Slate Press Ltd.
9 George St, Mt Eden
Auckland 1024, New Zealand
www.cleanslatepress.com

Author: Justin Brown
Edited by: Joy Cowley
Designed by: McGraw-Hill Australia Pty Ltd.
Illustrations by: Gaston Vanzet

Text © Justin Brown
Design and illustrations © McGraw-Hill Australia Pty Ltd. 2007
This edition published by Clean Slate Press Ltd. with the permission
of McGraw-Hill Australia Pty Ltd.
Originally published by McGraw-Hill Australia Pty Ltd. 2007

© This edition 2008 Clean Slate Press Ltd.

18 17 16 15 14 13
11 10 9 8 7 6 5 4

ISBN: 978-1-877454-55-4

Printed in China

Contents

1. MIKE AND THE WORLD GAMES

"Mike, look at my cabinet. It's empty," said Grandad. "I want you to go overseas and win some sports trophies for me."

"Cool!" said Mike. "Can I play softball and soccer? They're my favourites."

"No, I want you to play new sports you've never played before."

Mike Cool-as-You-Like put on his running shoes. "No worries, Grandad! There's no time to lose!"

The first thing Mike did was buy an airline ticket.

"One ticket to overseas, please," he said to the travel agent.

"Whereabouts overseas?" the travel agent asked.

"All of it, and chop-chop—I'm in a hurry," said Mike.

When Mike arrived in Tokyo, he was asked to fight Japan's champion sumo wrestler. Basho looked as though he had eaten too many pies at the school cafeteria. He was also wearing what looked like a big nappy. Mike laughed until he found out he had to wear one as well!

"Begin!" the referee yelled.

While Mike bit his fingernails, Basho, with the force and speed of a station wagon, ran towards him.

Before Mike had the chance to say, "Nice day," he was flattened like a pancake in the corner of the ring. Unfortunately, he'd eaten an enormous plate of sushi before the fight. He let out the biggest BURP you've ever heard.

"Give that man a trophy for his burping ability," squealed the ref.

Mike smiled, a little embarrassed, and wiped his mouth.

That night Mike took his trophy out for dinner, out to the movies and even out tenpin bowling. He was very proud of it. He was interviewed on Japanese television and asked how he managed to burp so well.

"Years of practice," said Mike. "But anyone can do it. You've just got to believe in yourself. BURP! Excuse me."

The next morning, Mike didn't eat any fruit for breakfast because he was off to the Big Apple—New York!

When he arrived, he was asked to play basketball. He'd never played before but was really excited to give it a go.

"I just hope I'm not a complete basket case," said Mike.

Near the end of the fourth quarter, Mike Cool-as-You-Like still hadn't touched the ball. With only seconds to go on the clock, the captain of the other side, Chuck Goober, got ready for a three-pointer that would win the game for his team. But as he was about to throw the ball, he saw Mike picking his nose. He missed completely.

Everyone laughed except Chuck.

"He put me off!" Chuck cried. "He was picking his nose!"

"Give that boy a trophy," said the coach. "He won us the game!"

The only skiing Mike had done before arriving in Switzerland was on the water. When he was handed some snow skis in the Swiss Alps, he was a bit worried.

"Don't worry," said the lady at the rental shop. "It's just like riding a bike."

This made Mike even more confused. "In that case, you'd better put training wheels on mine."

At the top of the mountain, Mike was told he'd be racing Sven Upandover, the fastest downhill skier in Europe. Sven was built like a gazelle and looked like the kid at school who always had the newest, most expensive clothes. At the starting line, Sven glared at Mike and spat his gum onto the snow.

"Good luck, Mr Learner Driver," he smirked. "You'll need it."

"On your marks!" yelled the umpire. "Get set! Go!"

They were off down the slopes, going faster than a robber in the night. But suddenly, out from the bushes came the biggest dog you've ever seen. Sven and Mike slid to a halt. The dog was heading for Sven, growling and showing its teeth. Now even though Mike

4

wasn't thinking of sending Sven a birthday present this year, he still felt he should do something about the dog that wanted a mouthful of Sven's pants. He made a huge snowball and hurled it. The snowball donked the dog right on the head, and it ran into the bushes, yelping.

"Give that boy a trophy for his snowball-throwing ability!" yelled Sven, who was as white as a ghost. "He saved my life!"

Everyone cheered, apart from Mike, who was busy making more snowballs in case the dog came back.

"Mike, my boy, how did you win all these?" Grandad asked, as he placed the trophies in his empty cabinet.

Mike was too ashamed to say by burping, picking my nose and throwing snowballs. "For … for being the best trier," he stammered.

"Yeah, right!" said his grandfather. "I read in the newspaper that you won them by burping, picking your nose and throwing snowballs!"

Mike decided to change the subject. "How about a game of softball, Grandad? You can bat."

2. MIKE EATS THE WORLD

Mike's grandfather said, "Mike, I'm sick of peanut and spaghetti omelettes. Why don't you travel the world, come home and cook me something unusual?"

"Like spaghetti with sausages?" asked Mike Cool-as-You-Like.

"No, something I've never tasted before."

"You got it, Grandad," said Mike grabbing his lunchbox. "I might even bring home a doggy bag."

Mike ordered a taxi and headed straight to the international airport. It was raining cats and dogs the whole way.

"Go through the puddles!" Mike said to the driver.

"My taxi will get all dirty."

"Stop being so grown-up," said Mike. "Dirt is fun!"

Grumble, grumble, went the taxi driver.

At the baggage check-in there was a line longer than the one for the school cafeteria. Everyone looked grumpy, including the security man who glared at Mike as if he was late and hadn't done his homework.

"You don't have a lot of stuff," he said, looking through Mike's backpack.

"Take half the clothes and twice the money, I always say," said Mike.

Three bags of peanuts and a dozen boiled eggs come up on the X-ray screen.

"What's this?" the security man frowned.

"Emergency supplies, in case I find overseas food too unusable," said Mike.

"Don't you mean unusual?"

Mike shrugged. "Whatever."

Mike Cool-as-You-Like got on the plane and flew to Thailand. At a street stall in Bangkok he asked to try the local dish.

"Yum!" said Mike, chewing. "Grandad's going to love this! What is it?"

"Deep-fried insects," said the waiter, smiling. "Most unusual."

"Hmm, tasty," said Mike, "very tasty and crunchy. But not as tasty and crunchy as spaghetti and peanuts."

Mike went back to his hotel room and made the biggest peanut and spaghetti omelette you've ever seen.

I'm hungry, thought Mike the next morning as he packed his bag. Luckily, his next stop was Hungary. He wondered if there were also countries called Peckish and Starving.

"Give me your national dish, Mr Hungry," he said to a well-dressed waiter with a pen behind his ear. "I need it for my grandad."

A dish arrived. Mike wasted no time eating.

"Delicious," he burped. "Very earthy. What are they?"

"Those, sir, are pig's trotters," said the waiter.

"Pig's wotters?" asked Mike.

"Trotters. You know, pig's feet."

"Hmm, tasty," Mike said, "very tasty and chewy. But the poor pigs! How will they get home! On the bus?"

The best thing about travel for Mike was the aeroplane. When grumpy adults asked how he coped with not showering, he answered, "I sleep in my clothes anyway. That way I never have to get dressed in the morning."

"I like my home comforts," an adult said.

Mike was ordering his fifth chocolate milk when he asked the flight attendant if he could ride up front with the pilots.

"The cockpit is for grown-ups only," the attendant said.

"I am grown-up!" said Mike. "I cut my own meat."

"All right then," said the flight attendant, smiling. "But just for a few minutes."

"Cool!" said Mike.

In the cockpit, it didn't take Mike long to act like a pilot. "Good evening, everybody," he said through the intercom. "This is Mike Cool-as-You-Like speaking. We are currently cruising at 28 million feet. On the menu today we have peanut and spaghetti omelettes and lollies for dessert. And if any groan-ups need to go to the toilet, they will have to put their hand up and ask."

Normally kids weren't allowed in the cockpit for landing, but for Mike Cool-as-You-Like the pilot made a special case. The plane touched down.

"Go through the puddles!" Mike yelled as they landed.

"My plane will get all dirty," said the pilot.

"Don't be so serious," said Mike. "It's fun!"

Grumble, grumble, went the pilot.

When Mike stepped off the plane in Zambia, he was wearing a gorilla suit so the monkeys wouldn't notice him. A man showed him to a table by the river. Mike hoped this would be the place where he'd find some really unusual food for his grandad.

"Yum!" He shrieked with delight when he tried a mouthful. "I love chicken!"

"I'm very glad you do," said the man. "What you're eating right now, however, is crocodile."

"Crocodile?" said Mike. "No, thanks! See ya later, Mr Waiter!"

Mike was really glad his grandfather had sent him around the world. It's not every day a kid eats a hamburger in Hamburg or a frankfurter in Frankfurt. But Mike missed home and his friends. What unusual dish could he make his grandad? All he wanted to cook were more peanut and spaghetti omelettes!

10

Mike's grandad had set the table for his return. "I've been looking forward to this, Mike," he smiled. "Unusual food, here we come!"

Mike didn't want to let his grandad down. He could go into the garden and cook insects like the ones in Thailand. But he couldn't face killing cute little beetles. Making fresh pigs' trotters like those in Hungary would mean his farm friends would never play soccer again. As for crocodile meat, the only crocodile he could find was a lime green, blow-up one in his neighbour's pool.

He didn't know what to do.

His Grandad winked at him. "I know what we could make," he said, pulling out some eggs, spaghetti and peanut butter from the pantry.

"Oh, my favourite!" said Mike.

Moments later, they sat at the table and smiled at each other, oozy peanut butter and spaghetti dripping from their mouths. "My favourite too, to be honest," said Grandad.

3. MIKE'S SPECIAL DELIVERY

"Mike," said Grandad. "I need you to do me a favour."

"Shoot, Grandad," said Mike.

"I need you to take this big suitcase to my brother Jimmy in Tipperary. It's a long way away, across the seas and over the land. You mustn't lose this suitcase. It is very important."

"10-4, rubber ducky," said Mike. "But what's in the suitcase?"

"I'll give you a clue. I like my brother and I have a lot of time for him."

Before Mike's big trip, serious adults had loads of advice.

"Don't talk to strangers," said one.

"Don't drink the water," said another.

"Learn some important phrases in Spanish, German and French, in case you get into trouble," said a third.

All good tips, thought Mike. That afternoon he learned how to say, "One chocolate milk, please," in Spanish, German and French.

Mike could barely pick up his grandad's huge suitcase, but eventually he put it in the trunk of a taxi and headed for the ferry terminal. He loved boats and had always dreamed of being a captain.

"Bumpy, isn't it?" a groan-up said to Mike.

"It's great fun," said Mike, finding a comfy position on his suitcase.

"But it's cold, not like being home in front of the fire."

"Where's your sense of adventure?" said Mike.

Grumble, grumble, went the adult.

Once ashore, Mike asked a porter to help with his suitcase.

"Whoo-ah!" said the porter, sweating as he lifted. "What's in here? A ton of rocks?"

"I don't know," said Mike. "But whatever it is, it's really important."

As the porter heaved the suitcase on the connecting train, Mike thanked him and started to walk off.

"Hey, fella," said the porter. "What about my tip?"

"Tip?" asked Mike.

"Yeah, I nearly did my back in carrying your suitcase! I think I deserve a tip."

Mike thought, then said, "Don't flick the newspaper while your dad's reading it."

Just as Mike had settled in his seat, a big hairy train conductor told him his suitcase was too big for the first-class carriage.

"Carry on luggage only," he spat, bits of leftover lunch leaving his teeth. "Put the bag in the goods carriage with the rats and cockroaches."

"But I need to look after it," said Mike. "It's really important that I don't lose it."

"Oh, well," the conductor said, grinning. "Say 'Hi' to the rats for me!"

The goods carriage was cold, dark and damp. Mike stepped over scurrying cockroaches and hoped not to find a rat. In the corner of the carriage was an old man sitting on a reclining chair.

"Are you an armchair traveller?" Mike asked the old man.

"I certainly am," he replied. "They put me in the goods carriage because my feet are too stinky. Will you stay and keep me company?"

"Of course!" said Mike. "We can swap travel stories!"

The company of rats and cockroaches and stinky feet kept Mike awake all night. He couldn't get off the train soon enough. But Grandad's really important suitcase was safe. Mike asked a porter to carry it to the bus station. The porter moaned and groaned and, with the help of two other men, heaved the suitcase onto a bus.

"Don't I get a tip?" he asked, when he saw Mike trying to find a good seat.

Not another one, thought Mike. Oh well! "If you offer to do the dishes, you'll get out of doing your homework," he said.

Over the next week, Mike pulled the huge suitcase through railway stations, across pedestrian crossings, down narrow streets and up steep hills. Sometimes he just had to stop and rest in a cafe with a massive jug of chocolate milk.

"What's in the bag?" serious adults asked.

"Really important stuff," he replied.

"Where are you heading?" one said.

"Tickleberry."

"Don't you mean Tipperary?"

"Whatever," said Mike.

When Mike arrived in Tipperary, it was pouring with rain. Mike was just glad, after all the travel and sleepless nights, to be here at last. But with no porters in sight, he had no choice but to drag the suitcase to the address his grandad had given him.

Out of breath, and looking like a drowned rat, he found the house he was looking for. He knocked on the door.

"Mike, you made it!" yelled his grandad's brother, giving him the biggest bear hug you could ever imagine.

"Great-Uncle Jimmy, I have a very important suitcase for you from Grandad," said Mike. "And there's a message. Grandad said he's got a lot of time for you."

"I'm thinking you'd better open the suitcase for me," said Great-Uncle Jimmy.

Slowly, Mike unlocked the huge suitcase. Inside was a heavy woollen blanket, which he unwrapped. Then he unwrapped a puffy feather quilt.

"A big clock!" Mike exclaimed.

"Not just any clock," said Great-Uncle Jimmy. "A grandfather clock!"

Mike still looked confused.

Great-Uncle Jimmy smiled. "To be sure, didn't your grandad tell you he had a lot of time for me?"

It took Mike a while to figure it out, but when he did, he laughed so hard it hurt.

4. MIKE THE HANDYMAN

Just as Mike Cool-as-You-Like was leaving Tipperary, he received an email from his grandad. It read:

Mike, there are a few things that need fixing before you come home. I need an engineer in France, a plumber in Venice and a builder in England. So hop on a boat as soon as you can. The new London Bridge is falling down and you're the man to fix it.

Mike emailed back. *No problem, Grandad! Always thought I was a bit of a handyman!*

As soon as Mike arrived in London, he visited a hardware store. "The new London Bridge is falling down," he said to the shopkeeper. "What will I need to fix it?"

"A miracle!" said the shopkeeper.

"Okay, said Mike. "I'll have a miracle—and a bag of nails."

"Why don't you paint Big Ben while you're at it!" smirked the shopkeeper.

"Don't be silly," said Mike. "I'm only here till tomorrow."

Mike studied his map and followed his nose to the new London Bridge. Once there, he got out his tool set and put on his hard hat.

"You'll never fix it," mumbled a very serious adult.

"It's on its last legs," said another.

"Build a bridge and get over it," said Mike. "I've got work to do!" He pulled out his drill set, his hammer and his nails.

Soon a whole bunch of Londoners on their way to work started helping. One, a man called Jack, said to Mike, "The old London Bridge was sold to America. We have to make sure we keep this one. We want our grandkids to see it."

"Don't worry, Jack," said Mike, putting in the last nails. "London Bridge is now open for business. Just don't break it again."

Mike had never been on a train that went underwater, but that's exactly what he did in the Chunnel on his way to France. When he arrived in Paris, he ate snails for lunch.

"Where might I find the Rifle Tower?" he asked a woman.

"Don't you mean the Eiffel Tower?"

"Either one," said Mike. "Grandad said it needs some work done."

"Don't we all!" said the Frenchwoman, pointing Mike in the right direction.

At the bottom of the tower, a man flapped about like a mad chicken. He ran towards Mike. "Mike Cool-as-You-Like!" he yelped. "Thank goodness you're here! My name is Pierre. The lift to the tower is broken! Can you fix it?"

"Relax, Pierre," said Mike. "Life's full of ups and downs. Let's have buttery croissants, camembert cheese and lemon soufflé. After that, we'll get to work."

Later, as they climbed the 1665 steps of the Eiffel Tower, Mike realised how lucky he was to have eaten a big lunch. He and Pierre both let out a large burp when they reached the top.

"I think I see the problem," said Mike, sitting on top of the lift. "There's a bird's nest in the cables."

"Would the birds mind moving to a nearby tree?" asked Pierre.

Mike laughed. "Even better, Monsieur, I'll put them into the canopy above that bistro. They can sing beautiful French songs for the customers!"

Next on Mike's "Handyman Tour" was the city of Venice. Mike liked the sound of Venice because it rhymed with tennis. He always found things easy to remember when they rhymed with something. Luckily for him, the man who ran the local hardware store was called Dennis.

"Dennis," said Mike. "Venice is leaking. If you don't sell me your biggest bath plug, your city will go down the gurgler."

"Sorry," said Dennis, "only my wife Glenys knows where the bath plugs are."

"Well, where's Glenys?" asked Mike.

"At tennis," said Dennis.

A short time later, with the world's biggest bath plug in his pocket, Mike waved down the nearest gondola. The man rowing had the longest oar Mike had ever seen. "I've noticed," Mike said to him, "you have no cars at all in Venice."

"That's because the city is on canals," said the man, rowing. "There are no cars, only boats. We don't even have traffic lights."

"So you can't get car sick!" said Mike. "Cool! I want to move here!"

Mike could hear the water slurping out of the canal as they approached. The crowd cheered when they saw his big bath plug. "Come on, everyone!" he said, jumping into the water. "The more the merrier!"

The kids dived in first. They splashed, bellyflopped and back-flipped. Meanwhile, the groan-ups dipped one foot in first, then the other, shivering as they went.

"Just dive straight in!" yelled Mike.

Grumble, grumble, went the adults.

Everyone tried to help Mike plug the hole at the bottom of the canal.

"My hands are filthy!" moaned a serious adult.

"Disgusting!" complained another.

"A bit of dirt never hurt!" said Mike.

After one more dive Mike found the hole, plugged it, and the water stopped.

"How can we ever thank you?" the mayor asked.

22

"Just make sure it doesn't happen again," said Mike. "And remember what your mum always said—don't waste water!"

"Grandad, I'm so glad to be home," said Mike collapsing on his grandfather's couch. "I need the coldest glass of chocolate milk ever tasted."

"Not so fast, Mike," said his grandad, going into the kitchen. "My toaster is broken. Since you're such a great handyman, would you be able to take a look at it for me?"

"Grandad, you must be joking!" said Mike.

"Yep, I am," Grandad said, and he passed him the coldest glass of chocolate milk ever tasted.

From the author

One day, I sat down at my computer to write a kids' story, while my one-year-old daughter, Sophie, slept in the next room. I had done all sorts of writing before, but this was the first time I wanted to write something just for me! I thought that if I laughed writing it, kids would laugh reading it.

Well, something must have gone right that afternoon, because within minutes, Mike Cool-as-You-Like popped out, fully formed! I liked him right from the start. I liked where he took me. Most of all, I loved how he got to do things I was never allowed to. After I finished that first story, I was about to celebrate by guzzling the biggest glass of chocolate milk you've ever seen … but Sophie needed her nappies changed!

For *Mike Cool-as-You-Like: Around the World,* I thought of all the places I'd like to see, and all the people I'd love to meet—and got Mike to go for me!

Justin Brown

From the illustrator

I loved drawing the pictures for
Mike Cool-as-You-Like because …

I wish I could be like Mike!
Just for one day would be okay
So that everything you say
Turns out your way!
To tip things upside down—
Who cares if groan-ups frown?
Load it up, Mike, and give me a shot,
And while you're there, one with the lot!
Let's go crazy, let's have some fun,
But watch out: we might have to run!
Mike's world is cool and …
Mike is as cool as I like.

Gaston Vanzet